The Best Teacher in the World

by Bernice Chardiet and Grace Maccarone
pictures by G. Brian Karas

SCHOLASTIC INC.

New York Toronto London Auckland Sydney

For Cindy and Jane.
B.C.

For Bernice and Jordan.
G.M.

For Sue and Bennett.
G.B.K.

ISBN 0-590-43307-5

Copyright © 1990 by Grace Maccarone
and
Bernice Chardiet.
Illustrations copyright © 1990 by G. Brian Karas.
All rights reserved. Published by Scholastic Inc.
Produced by Chardiet Unlimited, Inc.
12 11 10 9 8 7 6 5 4 3 2   0 1 2 3 4 5/9

Printed in the U.S.A.   8

First Scholastic printing, September 1990

"Good morning, class," Ms. Darcy said. "Who would like to take this note to Mrs. Walker?"

Everyone wanted to go.
Ms. Darcy was the best teacher
in the whole world.
She was very pretty.
And she was very smart.

Martin Kafka waved his pencil case in the air.
Everything came out.
Brenda Wicker nearly fell off of her chair.
"I'll go," she said.
Bunny Rabissi raised her hand as high as
she could.
She wiggled her fingers.
"Ooh ooo ooo! Pick me, please."

"Bunny will go this time," said Ms. Darcy.
Bunny popped up from her seat.
She stood up straight and tall.
As she passed Brenda, Bunny felt a little
kick on her ankle.
But she was too happy to care.

Ms. Darcy gave Bunny the note.
It was on a yellow piece of paper.
The paper was folded in half.
It was not sealed.

Bunny walked across the room.
Bunny heard a whisper.
"Have a carrot, Bunny Rabbit."
Bunny knew it was Raymond.
He always made fun of her name.
Sometimes it made her cry. But not now.

Bunny was happy and proud.
She was taking a note to Mrs. Walker.
She held her head up high
and wore a big smile on her face
as she left the room.

Bunny closed the door behind her.
Then her smile went away.
Where was Mrs. Walker's classroom?
Bunny did not know.
Should she go back and ask?
No, she could not.
The others would laugh.
Ms. Darcy would think she was a dummy.
Bunny would just have to try herself.
She started to walk down the hall.

Mr. Sherman's class was next door.
Bunny already knew that.
Mr. Sherman's class and Ms. Darcy's class
got together for recess.

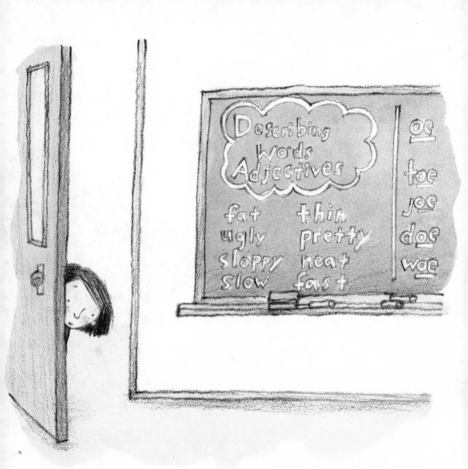

Ms. Stone's class was across the hall.
Bunny looked inside.
Everyone was copying from the blackboard.

The next door was closed.
Maybe it was Mrs. Walker's room.
Bunny opened the door.
She hoped no one would notice her.

But everyone did.
The teacher was Mrs. Kyle.
"May I help you?" she asked.
The whole class watched.
Bunny's face turned red.
Quickly she closed the door.

Bunny passed room after room.
She did not see Mrs. Walker.
Many of the doors were closed.
But she would not open them.
Not after she had made the mistake
in front of Mrs. Kyle's class.

Bunny walked up and down the hall twice.
She looked in the library.
She looked in the auditorium.
There was no sign of Mrs. Walker's class.

At last she went back to her
own classroom.
The back door was open.
Bunny waited outside
where no one could see her.

Ms. Darcy was reading about the ugly
duckling that turned into a swan.
It was one of Bunny's favorite stories.
Bunny wished she were inside.
She wished someone else had taken the
note to Mrs. Walker.
Bunny wanted to cry.

By now, the yellow paper was wrinkled.
What did it say?
Bunny knew she should not look.
But she had to.
Bunny read:

Nancy,
Meet me at Pine Street at four o'clock.
            Joyce

Bunny put the note in her pocket.
She walked back into the room.

"Did Mrs. Walker say anything?"
Ms. Darcy asked.
Bunny lied.
"She said okay."
Ms. Darcy smiled.
"Thank you, Bunny."

Bunny felt bad all afternoon.
She kept thinking about her fib.
She wanted to tell Ms. Darcy the truth.
But she didn't want Ms. Darcy
to think she was a dummy—
and now a liar, too.

Finally, the bell rang.
It was time to go home.
It was Bunny's last chance to tell
the truth but the words would not
come out.

That night, Bunny could not sleep.
She thought about Ms. Darcy.
Was she still waiting for Mrs. Walker
on Pine Street?

Bunny did not want to go to school the
next day.
"Your eyes do look a bit red," said her mom.
So Bunny stayed home.
Mom took the day off from work.
They played checkers and cards
and Candyville.
It should have been fun.
But it was not.
Bunny felt like a fibber and a fake.
Tomorrow she would go to school.

The next morning, Bunny looked for
Ms. Darcy in the schoolyard.
"I have to tell you something," said Bunny.
"I didn't give your note to Mrs. Walker."
"I know," said Ms. Darcy.
"I saw her in the parking lot after school.
But you were very brave to tell me."
Ms. Darcy gave Bunny a hug.
"Just promise me one thing," she said.
"Never be afraid to ask a question
when there's something you don't know.
All right?"

"Yes," said Bunny.
And she hugged Ms. Darcy back.
Ms. Darcy was the best teacher
in the whole world.
She was very pretty.
And very, VERY smart.